BROKENNEDY

Broken and Needy

Kezia Arterberry

Order this book online at www.trafford.com
or email orders@trafford.com

Most Trafford titles are also available at major online book retailers.

Printed in Victoria, BC, Canada.

ISBN: 978-1-4269-3210-6 (sc)
ISBN: 978-1-4269-3211-3 (e-b)

*Our mission is to efficiently provide the world's finest, most comprehensive
book publishing service, enabling every author to experience success.
To find out how to publish your book, your way, and have it available
worldwide, visit us online at www.trafford.com*

Trafford rev. 06/02/2010

 www.trafford.com

North America & international
toll-free: 1 888 232 4444 (USA & Canada)
phone: 250 383 6864 ♦ fax: 812 355 4082

Dedicated to
My mother, Rutha Arterberry

Preface:

This book was written to tell a story about a young girl that deals with being in a broken relationship. There are a lot of teenage girls who have dealt with similar situations in getting their heart broken. The main character struggles to heal emotionally, after what her ex-boyfriend did to her. She remains in denial, and hasn't really learned the difference between a fairytale romance, and real love.

Acknowledgments

There are several people that I would like to acknowledge. I would like to give a special thanks to my mom for supporting me, and helping me write this book. She has listened and made necessary suggestions to help make my writing better. I am forever thankful for her. I'd also like to acknowledge my best friends Jasmine Richerdson and Tori A. Sims, they have both been huge inspirations for me. They've inspired in their unique ways to take the gift of writing, that God has blessed me with and to put it to use. I have watched them both achieve many things, and it gave me the "go ahead" to write this book. There are two other very special people that I'd like to thank; Velma Hamilton, and Dorcus C. Chandler. They both mean so much to me. Velma Hamilton is not only my 'granny' but she is also my Pastor, Sunday school teacher, and mentor. Dorcus C. Chandler is also my mentor, and I really do look up to her. Her words of encouragement, her stories, and her advice, has helped me grow as a person. I just want to say that I love and thank God for each of you.

Foreword

Love Blinds. Fairytales are fairytales. Nothing more, nothing less. Kalldah Sharee Farland has suffered emotional abuse from the love of her life. Her heart has been broken, by him, time and time again. It is a constant struggle for her to heal emotionally. She tripped and fell into what she thought was love, but was only lust. She became blind to reality. The guy she thought truly loved her only wanted one thing. Sereyva Melone, and many others tried to help Kalldah see the truth. Kalldah came close, and then was suddenly dragged back into the same lies she'd been in before. It caused her much pain and heartache. This time she became so depressed, it seemed all hope was lost. Through all this, Sereyva learned what it is to be broken and needy. Though Kalldah suffered emotionally, she helped open the eyes of her friend, so she'd see how love blinds.

Broken and Intense L.O.V.E

The road has become narrow
And every edge stricken
With every curve is temptation
With every fault there's no compensation
So belittle every accent
Every inch of perfection, so profound
Every picture perfect fantasy
Turn to your beloved majesty

Here is to intense and find no comfort
Not quite the exaltation it was intended to be
A story of two friends turned into lovers
Their journey uphill and downhill
The stumbles and the falls
The accidental circumstances

Crossing forbidden boarders
Expressing intimate affections
Specializing at love's demise
Understanding l.o.v.e at every wits end
Knowing its ups and downs and misunderstandings
Crossing paths with its enemy, hate

Beautiful turned ugly
Arts mistake a masterpiece
Losing sight of the true prize
The bright blue skies, and all the flashing lights
Witness its cruel intentions first hand
Experience a new revolution

Like a newborn, street project
Like a journal of blank pages, waiting to be filled
An empty wine glass, left on a table in a bar
The instrumental without the lyrics
The movie without the credits

Six months later, looking back on it
The memories here for eternity
Runaway, to escape, travel around California
Open mouth, but no words left to say
Yet running through the mind as a maze
All the unanswered questions
The denial builds, as the raindrops poor
Earthquakes come and shakes up the earth
Unstable but built
The walls tremble and fall down
As the flames of love die out

Wonder if it's possible to stop
And then begin again?
Or just put the car in neutral and leave it be?
Causing the tumultuous thing to remain in its place
With time it gives way
Realize the truth
In my story things change gears
They begin rolling downhill

The dynamics of l.o.v.e
Become the necessity
The uprising of every girls dream
Need be it like the fairytales once read
Fiction turned bio and autobiographical
Fairytale expected to become reality

A love that once subdued
Now it no longer pursues
But leaves half empty, unfulfilled
No longer is there a purpose, no need to hang around

Turn the page to the next chapter of this life
Exit out of complete damnation
Forfeit the broken hearted alternative
Fast forward to the brighter side of life
Where the clouds dance with the horizon
The sun and the moon shine together
One goes down as the other rises up
Dance the night away
Without sinking to the ocean floors

Get a leave of absence
But one that lasts for eternity
Maybe forbid love in thy dwelling altogether
Because those past experiences never leave
Not held against, but definitely not forgotten

That one that use to be something special
It was altered and not wise
Doubled pleasure, gone
Doubled fun, gone
Over, done, finished, complete
Pressure puts on a love fest
This test is at the risk of one's survival

No study guide, no nothing
Blind to warnings, is blind to reality
The reality of broken love, intense emotions
This is the story of a broken and intense love.

Introduction:

We tend to devote all our time to assuaging our heartaches. They say that pain is weakness leaving the body, but I object. Pain is all in the mind. It's a mental illusion, capturing your vulnerability. I like to think that we each have a remote, and all you have to do is press the button, on and off. You determine the length and compatibility of it all. Pain is only capable of devouring emotions. It doesn't cause death, or anything else, except...

Weakness is tried by the depth of all your pain. Pain is at the expense of the inner man. The sting of death isn't what hurts, but it's the reality or thought of the past, present, or future. Anyone who is ready to depart will transition smoothly, entering into the gates of eternity. If they are uncertain that their destination will be glorious, then they will be hesitant and most likely having to be snatched away from the land of the living. So pain and suffering is at our own demise. It challenges our strengths and weaknesses. The power to control it comes from within.

I lost my best friend when I was sixteen. She did not die, but she did attempt suicide by slitting her wrists. I claim it a miracle that her mama found her in time. Danger truly was in her own hands, at her own will. Obviously not much thought was put into it. Kalldah

Sharee Farland is her name, and she was only seventeen. I witnessed her uprising and downfalls first hand. But never did I see suicide coming.

Love is viewed as the opposite of hate. Not in this story. Love is what caused Kalldah's pain and heartache. Day in and day out she suffered, but love was not alone. Jealousy, pride, faulty ambition, and of course cheating and deceit are known to associate with love, having a negative effect on its victim.

He looked into her eyes, and told her many lies. She was faulty and not wise. I stood by her side, encouraging her as she devoted all her time to him. The undeserving male, failed to commit. Strangely enough, she was fooled by his wit. She dedicated her deepest thoughts to him, that he practically owned a part of her heart.

Now that heart is void. The muscle has been weakened. It's been broken down, and torn apart, and shredded into a million pieces. For the work of this heartless man is as an art. He has been crowned with an elegant crown of his royalty. He is just one of the single princes in this palace. The palace where love and hate are con-joined. The feeble and the weak are crushed and buried beneath it all. The game of love is simply survival of the fittest.

I shed a tear at the thought of Kalldah... Being bound by the chains of deceit. Bolted down by defeat. Lies and selfishness surrounding her. She cries for help, but no one hears. Love blinds, not just the victim, but those around too. They're blinded by the fake smile, and the fake laughter. And all the materialistic things that crown him king. There's a reason for the p.i.m.p and his gold-diggin female friend.

As it appears, I am full of anger. I feel the pain of my friend, Kalldah. We were very close. One look in her eye tells the story, her story. The torment she felt, the strife that she dealt. All of it is in her eyes. That faded glow, the emptiness of her soul. She's physically there, but her mind is adrift. Her mental estate is asunder. But I have good news, for the storm is passing over. I once heard the teacher say, "Trouble won't last always."

Chapter one

Secretly, I dreaded visiting Kalldah at the rehabilitation facility. The treatment center happened to be located in Paradise Valley, also known as PV Medical Center. It is rather selfish of me to say, but I strongly dislike hospitals. The gloomy halls, the chilly flow from the air conditioning, and the light colors... I find it all depressing!

It was a long, dreary walk down the hall to Kalldah's room. Room 241. Once I reached her room, I peered through the tiny window at the header of the door. I saw Kalldah pacing around the room . As she paced around, she looked down, gazing intimately at a photograph of JD. Anger arose within me once I realized that she still had it. Multiple times, after her breakup, I tried persuading her to burn it as an act of closure. Seeing that this didn't go down, I abruptly pushed the door open, and stormed in. Kalldah stopped dead in her tracks, looking startled, she dropped the photo onto the floor. I saw fear lingering in her eyes. I bent down and grabbed the photo, and began waving it in Kalldah's face.

When Kalldah hurt, I hurt. No doubt I felt her pain. When she cried, I cried with her. Though I was nowhere near her when she attempted to take away her life... If you care about somebody enough, then their emotions will touch you. You'll do all you can to help lighten their heavy load, because you know that when they are gone, it's as if a part of you has gone missing.

"Why do you still have this?" I asked Kalldah coldly. I sat down in the leather chair next to her bed. She shrugged her shoulders, staring down at the floor with a look of guilt smeared upon her face. She said to me, "I don't know." I shook my head in frustration. "Kalldah, you need to let him go!" I demanded. "I know. I know," She said nonchalantly. "I think that I am not ready to let go yet. I mean...Sereyva it's not that easy!"

I took Kalldah's hand, and clasped mine upon hers. "Kalldah, you're not going to get out of here if you don't let that boy go! You know why? Because you'll end up right back here again. Or worse, you may end up dead!" "But I love him!" She argued. "No, you're in love with the idea of him! Kalldah, do you realize why you are here?" My eyes began to water. I tried so hard to hold back the tears, but I couldn't hold them back any longer. I had to let them flow.

"Look Sereyva, I got to get to my therapy session with Dr. McKay." And with that, Kalldah brushed pass me, and headed out the door. I stood up slowly, wiping the tears away from my eyes. I had not expected this little drama to take place. But how could I have expected it to have gone smoothly? Because, I had a little faith, and a little bit of hope that Kalldah would overcome this. This being a love turned into a mere tragedy. Refer to "Romeo and Juliet." That was a forbidden love, turned into a tragedy. Which is more realistic in the eyes of man? A Cinderella fairytale, or a tragedy of love to death?

Love is the one word that is used so loosely. Ever so common. So every time you say " I love you," you're willing to sacrifice your life for that person, place or thing?

Romeo and Juliet died, because their love for each other was forbidden. This makes sense in my eyes. Though it is a scary thing to admit.

How can love and hate possibly be opposites when they have something in common? There are people in this world who've taken the life of their enemy, and suffer the consequence. They too, are giving their life, because of hate. The consequence may be the death penalty, or being sentenced to life in prison, because of the crime they committed. Either way, it's safe to say that love and hate may be viewed as opposites, but they both have something in common.

Control. Love and hate. Either you control it, or you let it control you. Every night I pray for my dear friend. That she will let go of her past, and stop living in denial. Kalldah entered into Dr. McKay's office. Dr. McKay was searching through her file cabinet. When she heard Kalldah enter, she spun around in her chair and folded her arms on the top of her desk. "I was wondering when you'd arrive," She said amusingly, with a crooked smile on her face.

Dr. McKay's office was surprisingly dull. The blinds covering the windows were shut. The ceiling lights flickered, and were dim as can be. It was noticeably freezing at what seemed to be negative twelve degrees Celsius. Dr. McKay's office was a rectangular room with a desk parked in the north side corner on the left, and two chairs only two feet away from it. There was also a recliner positioned in the right corner, on the south side of the room, parallel to the desk. The walls were pale and bare. The paint nearly faded.

"I oblige. I had a visitor, and yea.." She drifted off. Kalldah shrugged her shoulders and sat down. "Did the

3

visitor happen to be Sereyva Melone?" "Sure it was. But it doesn't matter." Dr. McKay looked astonished. "I thought it would be nice for you to have someone come to visit you." Kalldah shook her head and said, "Not really." "How come?" questioned Dr. McKay.

"I don't need to be bothered by her. She came up here, and decided that she can tell me what to do. I can make my own decisions." Dr. McKay chuckled. "And look where that got you!" She exclaimed, spreading out her arms while looking over the room. "Kalldah you are here because you made a wrong decision." "Well, maybe it wasn't. It was planned. Not a mistake! I meant to do what I did. Too bad it didn't..."

"Too bad it didn't what?" Dr. McKay asked, interrupting Kalldah. "You tried to kill yourself Kalldah! What if your mama hadn't been there to get you help? You'd be gone! Okay? Once you're gone, you're not coming back!" Kalldah just shrugged her shoulders. Dr. McKay was obviously becoming irritated. Kalldah happened to be one of the most difficult patients that she had to work with.

"Okay Kalldah, listen to me. Let me help you. Explain to me why you did what you did." Kalldah stared at the floor. Moments later she finally spoke. "Love happened. Okay? I met this guy. I thought he was the world. You know, something special. Mama always told me to be careful, to wait. But I was foolish to ignore her. See I thought things would be different for me. JD was this sweet, charming prince. He had this slick way to make me feel worth the world and more. Whenever we talked, or were in a crowded room together, he had a way of making me feel as if I was the only human who existed. Not only that, but we dated for eight months. It was my first relationship ever. He'd buy me jewelry, chocolate, balloons, roses for anniversaries and some holidays. Then he told me he loved me." Kalldah began to choke, as tears began streaming down her face. "I remember it so vividly. It's as if it happened yesterday. He held me close, and told me he'd never let me go. He laid a kiss upon my lips, and whispered in my ears. He said, 'I love you Kalldah Sharee Farland. One day we'll get married, and have a family. You're my girl now and forever.' Those words were nothing but pure lies. I never gave myself up to him, because I wanted it to be special. But I loved him, and I still do. I believed him. That was my mistake."

Dr. McKay sighed, and leaned back in her chair. Kalldah wiped her face, blew her nose, and waited to hear what McKay had to say. "Kalldah. No boy or man is worth your tears. You can't control how you feel about someone. But you can misinterpret what love is. Until you realize this, and believe that your feelings for JD aren't love, then you can't heal." Kalldah looked confused. She asked, "If it wasn't love then what was it?" "Infatuation," Dr. McKay replied.

Love is blinding. What does it take to open the eyes of a blind man? It takes love to open the eyes of a blind man. For love is natural, and uncontrollable. It wraps itself around you. Then it leads you astray to toils and snares. It forces itself upon you, and pulls you down into the bottomless pit. Darkness surrounds, chills run down your spine. You try earnestly to awaken out of this dream. Instead you awaken to reality. Finally you realize that things aren't really what they seem.

The logistics of it all is almost unbearable. The logic is the truth, and the truth is all that can set you free. Freeing you from the torment. Its own psych-analogist is present.

Strictly you are the victim, and love is your enemy? No! Love is your friend, and hate is your enemy. So while I talk about love, I am talking about hate. Hate destroys. It takes down a love that was once built.

Your weak, and just not strong enough. Not wise enough to know the difference. There is a difference, because they are opposites of each other. You are in complete desperation. And all this does is challenge your continuity. I'll tell you once, but not twice... Leave it alone. I will tell you to let it go, break free. Release yourself, set yourself free. Find the victory in this mess. You've been under false pretenses that are no longer valid. Complete and utter destruction is not the answer. The best alternative you have, this day, is to breakthrough.

Breakthrough to the other side, the better things in life. People may let you down, but the worse crime you could possibly commit in this case, is letting your own self down.

I'm almost positive that none of this makes much sense. This is not my story, its Kalldah's. She is not strong enough to tell it, but I am. It's nothing but a testimony, and I'm her witness.

One thing that you must know is that this truth is liable. The facts will remain facts, and lies will remain lies. There are visibly two sides to this. This open-ended subject is... Love is beautiful, and hate is ugly. Hate is love's enemy. Though love may be binding, it is one of the best things one could ever experience. Falling in love.

"Umm... Doctor, I'm pretty sure it wasn't infatuation. I tried to kill myself remember? It had to be love!" "Had to be?" Dr. McKay asked Kalldah questioningly. "Yes. I mean...Wasn't it?" "Kalldah, honey, it's clear to me that you aren't sure yourself." "But doctor! If it isn't love, then how can it possibly be infatuation? I mean, you telling' me this as if you know exactly how I feel. But you don't! You didn't try to commit suicide. I did!"

Dr. McKay folded her arms against her chest, took a deep breath, and then let it out slowly. "Your right, I don't. What I do know is that you clearly cannot see where you drift. Your blind to the reality of all this. And yea, it sucks! But I've been doing my job for twelve years now. Trust me, I know what I am talking about. What I need you to do is listen. Just listen." "Sure. Okay," Kalldah hesitated, and then continued. "So what is this infatuation thing?"

Standing on the outside looking in. Balancing your weight on the tip of an ice berg. The chances of you falling are beyond belief. The majority of human beings fail to realize the truth of this. The bearable and the unbearable, like a lamb being slaughtered. You count your many blessings, failing to see your dream. First you say yes, and then you begin marching towards your destiny.

What you need is a savior to rescue you before it's too late. Before the broken pieces of your heart are hand held. Which is after you've opened up your heart, for the entire world to see? Exposing even the most unintentional flaws. And you wish you could erase them all. By then it's too late. You've already reached your fate. Now your bitter and full hate. Love blinds. It was clear at first sight, but Kalldah said to herself, before me, before all this happened... "But I love him!"

She thought I wouldn't understand. But what she called love, I was able to comprehend. So hatred's arms are spread out wide. He welcomes you to "The Broken Hearts Club."

It's Gone

I don't have a broken heart anymore
It don't hurt to look at you anymore
I just go around doing my own thing
I don't have to wipe away any tears

It's not like it use to be
Every time I saw you I'd shed a tear
I can just go through my day
Won't even have to say a word about you

And I don't live to shed my tears
I don't cry because I want you
It's just the fact that I don't have to deal
My broken heart has been mended

Don't have to feel sorry for myself
Don't have to live ashamed
Don't have to live with so much guilt
When I'm innocent
My broken heart is gone

Don't have to look you in the eye
And feel that I'm losing you
Don't have to be by your side
Wishing I was with someone else

My broken heart is gone.

Chapter Two

"Infatuation is being in denial. Kalldah, it's not love at all, nor is it hate. But it is only lusting towards the object of your affections. It is just a realization of your attraction to a man. Though your heart may beat faster, your heart is not in it. It's the natural desire for someone. The difference between love and infatuation is this: Lack of an emotional connection. I'm going to make it sweet and simple. You love his body, not him." Kalldah squinted her eyes, and glared at Dr. McKay. A broad smile spread across Dr. McKay's face, as she began to shutter with laughter.

Kalldah cleared her throat and said, "How embarrassing is this?" Her cheeks began to burn. "I know. I know. Of course you're going to want to deny it. But once you come to terms with what this really means, then you'll be alright." Kalldah chuckled to herself, and mumbled, "How do you know this?" I can't convince you, all I can possibly do is hope that you'll trust me on this one."

Kalldah suddenly stood up and walked towards the door. "Okay doctor. So I'll be seeing you soon." Dr. McKay raised her left eyebrow. "How soon exactly?" she asked. "The day after tomorrow I suppose." "Wednesday we shall resume," agreed Dr. McKay.

I contemplated multiple times, whether or not I should go visit Kalldah. I wouldn't be having second thoughts, or first thoughts if it were a different story. If Kalldah was lying in a hospital bed, as helpless as can be, then sure. Sure, I would be by her bed side day and night. Day in and day out I would physically be there for her. However, this is not the case. Instead, Kalldah has slim to none advantages. Every conversation involving her tends to be awkward.

You can give, and give, and give, and receive nothing in return. Absolutely nothing. She's like a mirror image. Simply a reflection of her pain and sorrows. Think of it this way; If someone is sad, they won't prance around with a ridiculous grin upon their face. At least I don't know of anyone who would.

The reason for Kalldah's insincerity is because she's emotionally suffering. Perhaps she's a bit mentally unstable. Okay, this sounds harsh. Yet, if you only knew firsthand what it's like... Selfish. I'm being completely selfish. Instead of being understanding of these troubling circumstances, I'm being overly judgmental.

Lesson learned: Be more understanding of others. Pretty simple isn't it? Well, I oblige. Like I said, lesson learned, I'm going to see the Kalldah. Tomorrow.

Kalldah opened the door before I was able to knock. "Sereyva!" Kalldah greeted me with a hug. "Why are you s...sss...so enthusiastic to see me?" I stuttered, gasping for breath. Her hug was a tight squeeze. "I didn't think you'd come," She hastily replied. We shuffled over to her bed and sat down. We didn't exactly sit down. It was more like dropping down! Anyway, we both just stared down at the floor in silence.

I sighed loudly. "So... How have you been?" I asked. "Fine. I've been going to see Dr. McKay. That's where I went the last time you came, and earlier today." "Are you progressing at all?" "Well, I'm actually listening to what she has to say if that's what you mean. I'm sorry Sereyva." "What for?" I asked. "You know, I didn't exactly hear you out on Monday. I treated you rather rudely. It wasn't right. I should have listened." "Well, I'm not a licensed doctor either," I said sarcastically. She laughed. "Yes that's true. But you're my friend. I should be quick to listen to you than some stranger." "She's no stranger Kalldah." "Ahh... You know what I mean."

I yawned, and took a look around the room. "How long do you have left in this dump aye?" "One, this is not Vancouver. Two, really soon. Dr. McKay say's I have to heal emotionally first."

One week later, late one afternoon, there came a knock on Kalldah's room door. Kalldah arose from her bed and dragged herself to the door. "Yes?" She asked lazily. A dark skinned, African girl, with two long, thick dreads hanging down her back, stood at the door. Kalldah's eyes widened as she looked the girl up and down.

The girl looked to be fresh out of high school. She was lengthy, and slender, with scars. A part of her appeared to be flawless, but the scar that stretched wickedly across her forehead and over her left eye seemed to signify weakness. Weakness doesn't signify who a person is. It only represents a struggle. Though she was slender, she was naturally built. Not as one who'd work out though. But definitely the opposite of a scrawny, tinge, frail, little girl. The girl appeared to be one with a hidden talent. Maybe she could lift, and hold a body on the tip of her pinky finger. No! She couldn't possibly do such a thing. It's nearly impossible to make a reasonable assumption about this girl.

Yet just looking at her standing there, you could tell that she had a story. Something had happened.

"This is room 241 correct?" She asked.

"Yes it is," Kalldah replied.

"Then this is my room," she said bluntly, brushing past her.

The girl sat her suitcase down, pulled off her jacket, and laid it across a chair. Kalldah stared at the girl, watching her every move. Finally she said, "You're the first roommate I've had since I've been here." "I don't want to be here," she said automatically. Kalldah hesitated, and then responded. "I don't either." She just rolled her eyes, and began unpacking her suitcase. Kalldah sat down on her bottom bunk, and watched quietly.

"Can I at least know your name?" Kalldah asked.

"Trinity," she replied.

"I'm Kalldah. Kalldah Farland. So ummm... How long are you here for?"

"Why you ask me questions? Do I ask you questions?"

"I'm just trying to be polite. At no means am I looking for a dispute!"

Trinity dropped her clothes, and clasped her hands on her face. While shaking her head she said, "Oh god! I've done it again!" She yelled. "What?" Kalldah asked curiously. One of the nurses came and stuck her head in the room, and asked "Is everything alright in here?"

Kalldah looked at Trinity. Trinity laughed and nodded her head yes. "Alright," the nurse said and left. "Kalldah girl! I really don't want to be here. I was moved out of "Juvy", because my old roommate and I fought. We got into it pretty bad."

Somewhere deep down, built in the inner-structure of her heart, she realizes the truth. Denial is simply that wicked demon that won't let her alone. How easy is it for one to lie to them self. To make them self's believe all the things they wish were true. It's only lies man! Only lies. Theres no truth to be found. Being lost in a world of uncertainty is hell all by itself. Waiting for your fairytale to begin, but it never will.

Looking for something that can never be found. Wasting away your days with meaningless hope, full of obscurities. Thinking that prince charming will come riding towards you in the moonlight. Instead, he'll pull out a knife, and take away your life. For fairytales will remain fairytales. They'll become nothing more.

If your name and his is written in the stars, well there are only two conclusions for it. One, it's a coincidence. Two, it's just your imagination. Nothing more than a temptation running away with thee. The Temptations themselves admit it. To you it's a simple melody. To me it is reality.

Love blinds. It creates an illusion. Receiving you unto itself. Selfishly taking ownership of you. Sometimes it gives back to you... What you give is what you get. What you got is what you gave. Sometimes more, but often less. Though some have success with love, there are those who don't. Some are fooled and later lost. If love wasn't blinding, then it couldn't be binding. Marriage proves this theory. It speaks for itself. Divorce is only a flame of love finally burning out. There's a reason for it all. Lovers don't know what it takes to keep the fire burning.

Still, deep down somewhere in Kalldah's heart, she knows this. But she doesn't know it as the truth. May it be too late to compromise with fate. Love can be beautiful, but hate can destroy. Every night I pray, and every night I prayed. I pray that Kalldah will open her eyes wide enough to see that love has an enemy called hate. And what she calls love is only infatuation. Infatuation being one of hate's tricks in the book. Out to deceive those who stumble and fall... In what to them is love.

Love- To care for someone till death doth part you. Passion and emotion. Attraction to another. Not lust. Unconditional, and longsuffering.

"So Trinity... how badly were you injured?" Kalldah asked curiously. "Bad enough," Trinity replied. "I have a few scars and bruises here and there," she said, tracing over the left side of her forehead. Kalldah was not satisfied with her answer. "Come on, tell me more," Kalldah urged. Trinity rolled her eyes.

"Fine then! It was bad enough that I had to get stitches, okay?"

"Okay. How many?" Kalldah pried. Trinity switched from one facial expression to the next, making it obvious that this was a sore topic of discussion for her. But Kalldah pressed on.

"Three. Just three of them. One on the back of my head, but you can't see it, because of my hair. There's one on my forehead, and one on my hand." Trinity stretched out her arm in front of Kalldah, showing her, her fist. Kalldah surveyed her fist erratically.

"How'd you manage to get that on your hand?"

"Look. You can see how the scar goes down between my index finger, and trails down to my wrist." Trinity flipped her arm around so Kalldah could see.

"Dang! May I say that, that looks painful. When did you get stitched up?"

"Last night I went in. Then they had me stay the rest of the night for observation. While I was laying around the hospital, my mama was busy flipping through phone books, searching for a place that I could go. So here I am. What's with all the questions Kalldah?"

Kalldah stammered, "I...I...I..was ummm... I was just wondering is all. I'm sorry, I shouldn't be so nosy I suppose."

Trinity grinned and said, "Let's make this equal then. Now, it's your turn to tell me a little bit about you!" Kalldah frowned at the suggestion, as if her life's story was confidential. "Come Kalldah, let's hear it."

Kalldah blushed. "If I tell you, you will laugh," Kalldah declared. "That's what you think." "No," replied Kalldah. "That's what I know."

"Well excuse me, but I told you why I'm here, now it's your turn." Trinity looked furious. "Damn! Okay. No need for you to get all bent out of shape about it."

"It's only fair," replied Trinity.

"Love happened." Trinity stared at Kalldah with a blank face.

For how challenging could it be to explain that love happened? How do you tell someone that love was only lies, if your still in denial? You don't . Like Kalldah, you leave it be. Your mental escape becomes deformed as time flies by. Deep down your desperate, but no one hears your call for help. No-one hears Kalldah's inner cry for help.

"What do you mean, love happened?" Trinity asked.

"I fell in love," Kalldah said. Trinity glared at Kalldah, and questioned her. "What does love have to do with you being sent to rehab Kalldah?"

"He hit me. My ex lover hit me. I fell and got a concussion. When I got out of the hospital, my parents sent me here."

"May I ask why you remain? I mean, if you're no longer physically hurt and your done recovering, then why are you still here? Can't you leave now?"

"Soon, Trinity I will be out of here soon. I know I'm no longer suffering physically. But my Doctor says I'm mentally unstable. So I got to see my therapist daily. Dr. McKay is her name."

Trinity shook her head in confusion. "Okay, so you're telling me that you were abused? Then technically you are still recovering Kalldah. Only your healing mentally. You know, it's an emotional thing. Are you bipolar? Emotionally unstable at all?"

Now it was Kalldah's turn to be confused. "You are starting to sound like my doctor. I'm fine." "Kalldah, you and I both know that if we were fine, then neither one of us would be in this place."

These walls were built by her hands. This destructive masterpiece is her creation. They were handcrafted by the intellect of an innocent woman. A beautiful young lady to be exact. One who was vibrant, unveiling, zealous, and not selfish. She gave of herself to the very core. The core of her heart is what I mean. She deliberately disobeyed the standard laws of love. In my own words I quote, 'Never give your heart to a man if he is not worthy.' For every cause there is an effect. Again and again, I consistently rehearse into your memory, this. This is the reality of it all. She put herself here, into this place you see. Escaping is not a promise. When entering a relationship, love is not guaranteed. Who said that this man you love will love you back? Again, this is the reality of it all. Kalldah's reality. It is a shame that it's too late for Kalldah to take these words to heart.

One month later...

Monday.

"Kalldah you have a call waiting." Kalldah looked up from her book and saw Delhia, an assistant nurse, gazing down at her. "Oh, okay. Thanks."

Thanks." Delhia turned and began to walk away. "Wait!" Kalldah jumped up from her seat, and stopped in front of Delhia. "What is it?" Delhia asked startled. Kalldah laughed to herself, and said apologetically, "I'm sorry. But do you know who called?" "Uhh... I believe his name is Mr. Branson." Kalldah cringed when she heard the name.

On call.

"Hello."

"Kalldah! Finally I get to hear your voice. Longtime no see baby. How you been?"

"JD! Why are you calling me? And how did you get this number?"

"I wanted to hear your voice. Is that a crime?"

"Nooo... How did you get this number?"

"I got in contact with your parents, and they told me you were at PV. Aren't you happy to hear from me baby?"

"Don't call me baby! I don't have anything to say to you JD."

"Jesus! Kalldah calm down. How many times do I have to say I'm sorry?"

"JD, I don't care how many times you apologize. I refuse to except."

"Ahh... Come on Kalldah. You have to forgive me sometime baby," JD said cunningly.

"I told you to stop calling me that!"

"Don't disrespect me Kalldah!" JD's tone deepened.

"And what are you going to do huh? What do you want? Why did you call?"

"I wanted to hear your voice." He paused. "So we can talk."

"JD, I don't want to talk to you okay? I blame you for me being here. You put me here JD! You put me here. What could we possibly have to talk about?"

"Now don't be like that. There's no reason we can't get past this."

"How JD? How could we possibly get past this?"

JD did not hesitate to say, "Let's get back together." Kalldah nearly dropped the phone when she heard that. She didn't speak for a moment. Then she began to laugh abruptly.

"You... Do you really think that I would get back with you? You've got to be out of your mind! After what you did? If I can't bring myself to forgive you, why would I go out with you?"

"Because you love me."

Believable

We searched in other worlds
We looked in foreign dimensions
We went to another place
When the answers was right in our hands

And all that time we worried
When we could have laughed
Comforted one another and
Mended one another's broken hearts

But here we go, here we stand
This is only the beginning
No more time to waist
It's so believable, so believable

It's so dynamic
So strong
I can never let go

The more I try
The harder to find
What it is
Deep inside my heart

And here we go, here we stand
We got everything we've ever wanted
We don't need the whole world
To find love

Here we go, here we stand
This is only the beginning
No more time to waist, it's so believable.

Chapter Three

You and Your Highway

The highway of life is filled with so much strife
You got off track and can't find your way back
With all your heart, you want to deny the truth

You want to believe your past life was all a lie
Because you made so many mistakes
In people's eyes your nothing more than a fake

But wait!
It's not too late
Nobody can change your fate
As long as you survive, your dream will stay alive
What's in you will come out
So let no one make you or break you
Just prepare to break through
From the start, you should follow your heart

Every time you let your voice be heard
The people start complaining
But what they don't know, is that
Someday, your picture, they'll be framing
So stay in your lane
On your highway
Cause in the end, all that will matter
Is you.

It is not a bit surprising to me that once again, JD's words consumed Kalldah. As I stated before, it's too late for Kalldah to take these words, my words to heart. Never will she be able to go back and re-live the past.

I am not one to blame for this. She set herself up for what is to come all on her own. Many times I wonder if I could have done more to protect this from happening. But how can one woman, alone, prevent fate from happening? You can't. I was her friend. I stood by her side through everything I could. There is no way that I could have prevented her from making a complete disaster of her entire life in general.

I did what I could to help her. Those days I visited her in rehab...Soon the time came for me to stop. It was time for me to step aside and let her story play out.

If you close your eyes, you can picture this all in your head. Kalldah's story I mean. It's clearly in black and white. There's love and hate, life and death, the past and the future. It's all there. And somewhere deep down, there's an almost-fatal purpose for it all. I say all this, because Kalldah did the one thing I dared she not do. Kalldah was leered back into a faulty relationship with the one and only JD Branson. The notorious JD, once again, held Kalldah in the palm of his four fingered hand.

I know what JD's intentions were. I also know that his actions got him into plenty of trouble.

Wednesday. Two weeks after the call from JD.

Dr. McKay ushered Kalldah into her office expediently. " I have news for you Kalldah," McKay told Kalldah. Kalldah looked blank. She asked, "Is it good news or bad news?" "You don't need to worry," replied Dr. McKay.

"Then what is it?"

"Your parents have requested your release."

"Really? It's time for me to go?"

"No," Dr. McKay said hesitantly. "It's not. But we can't hold you against your parents will. This is rehab, not a jail cell. No matter how much it may feel like one."

"Well, I get to get out early and I am glad," Kalldah said triumphantly.

"Yes, but that doesn't mean that you are ready to leave. Your parents are making a huge mistake in letting you go so soon."

"But I thought I would be getting out of here soon anyways? What's the big deal?"

"The past couple of weeks have been good for you. Indeed, I have witnessed a huge amount of progress. You've come a long way Kalldah."

"Then why is it such a problem that I be released early?"

"You don't appear to be mentally stable yet Kalldah."

"Doctor please! My brain is functioning fine!"

"Very well. Yet your mentality is positioned incorrectly."

"Meaning?"

"Meaning, your still in denial."

"I am not."

"Fine. Prove it! Prove to me that you are no longer in denial. Kalldah I want you to talk to me. As of today, right now, this moment, how do you feel about JD?"

"I love him," Kalldah said quickly. She spoke freely, without hesitation. Dr. McKay on the other hand was as frustrated as can be. She wanted to restore sight to Kalldah's blind eyes.

"What do you mean you love him?" Dr. McKay asked.

"We got back together two weeks ago. We've been talking every day since."

Dr. McKay looked furious. "And your barely telling me this now? Kalldah! You mean to tell me that you've been coming here, sitting in front of me, practically lying to my face for two whole weeks? This is why you are not ready to leave. You've been lying to yourself. Now you're lying to me! I'm your counselor Kalldah. I'm here to help you, so I thought. But I can't help you if you're not straight up with me!"

"I'm sorry," Kalldah said quietly. "Do you have anything to say?"

"Yea. I want to be straight up with you. Now that you know."

"I'm afraid it's too late for you Kalldah. That's why your parents sent you here in the first place. So that I could help you. I've been available to you for three months now. Your parents are ready for you to be released. It's too late."

"And there's nothing that you can do to change their minds? Can't you tell them what you told me? About how I'm mentally unstable and stuff," Kalldah asked hopefully.

"I'm sorry, I can't. It's not my decision. You have to speak with them yourself."

"Oh."

"Kalldah, you being here is not free. It's not a cheap price either. Because you aren't here recovering from anything that has to do with an injury or a drug related cause. Your case is different. It's very special actually."

Kalldah was released from the Paradise Valley Medical Center later on that week. That was bound to happen sooner than later. I believe that even if Kalldah remained in rehab for a short while longer, she still would be in denial. Sometimes you cannot say or do anything to change the heart or mind of a single soul. Why? Because the heart has been hardened. Hardened from all the hurt and pain. She built a wall that surrounds her heart like a shield. A shield that is bullet' proof. She is trapped within the four walls that surround her heart. No longer does she hold the key, which can unlock the door to her hardened heart. She has become so weak, that she's lost all control. This for her is like a disease. The only cure is nourishment and enrichment in the knowledge of what true love really is. Cause all the signs and tells of love were only lies. There is no truth of that story existing.

Kalldah remained blind to the true facts of her love life. JD once again captivated her mind, and got from her what he wanted. He continued to whisper lies in her ear, and sweet talk her into giving...

She gave of herself, till she could give no more. Trust is what bonded the two together. Kalldah believed that things would be different this time. But I must ask, did she truly trust him? Maybe it was fear that led her to believe his lies. She'd been hurt before, and didn't want to be hurt again.

If she could just forgive and forget, or act as if he hadn't hurt her, then everything would be okay. That is not reality. It's being in denial. Denial is the one place you never want to be.

JD and Kalldah grew closer together, as their relationship, based on lies, lengthened out. The two "love birds" spent time with each other every day. JD made promises to Kalldah that any woman should know a man cannot keep. This failing love trend continued on, until something happened. Something happened that I am still trying to figure out.

Kalldah is one of those people who seem to always be caught up in some type of drama. Wherever she goes, it's as if a thunder storm is trailing her behind. Now I'm going to change gears, because there's an effect to love's cause. As I mentioned, I am still struggling to make sense of it all. But I said before, that this is Kalldah's story. Not mine. She is not strong enough to tell it, but I am. This is her testimony, and I am simply her witness.

Do not be confused. Though you may be led to believe that JD is the bad guy. Hate has its way of undermining it all. Making it seem like it's "fake" love is true love. I'm here to tell you that it isn't. You cannot trust whatever JD may do or say.

Now that I have warned you, I will continue...

Chapter Four

Kalldah leaned back against the door in mere hesitation. She could hear her deceased mother's voice in her ear, ushering her into a deep contrition. "Take a deep breath, and relax." Her heart began to pound against her chest, as she knelt against the wall. Her arms stretched out against the plastered cushion. The room was dark and hallow. Kalldah took a deep breath, and slowly let out the dusty oxygen, once inhaled.

Four hours later...

She jumped up, startled, hearing a loud bang on the door. "Kalldah are you in there?" asked a male, with a mellow, tenor voice. There was no answer."Kalldah I know you're in there! Come on, open up. Now!" Slowly Kalldah arose and cracked open the door just enough for a glimpse of sunlight to rush in and brighten up a corner of the room. JD pushed the door open, and made his way into the room, nearly trampling over Kalldah.

Kalldah regained her balance, and stepped backwards. Shivers ran up and down her spine, her eyes were glossy, and her skin was pale. Her hair was tangled in a mass. "Why are you here? I've been searching all over for you! What is going on?" JD questioned her, grabbing a hold of his girlfriends arm.

"Hiding," said Kalldah. "Hiding? What are you hiding?" He asked her. Kalldah gave him a blank stare. JD placed his hands on her shoulders and gave her an intense shake. "Kalldah," He said in a cunning, but persuasive tone. "I need you to work with me here. Okay? Tell me what is going on. I'm trying to help you." Kalldah shuttered and shut her eyes. "Kalldah! Kalldah! Kalldah? Kalldah!!!"

Kalldah stuttered, and these are the words she uttered: "Nothing. Hiding nothing. Interstate 64. I crashed Eric's BMW. Missing."

JD's eyebrows rose. "Who or what is missing? Kalldah please? Look me in the eye, and tell me the truth."

Kalldah opened her eyes. Dazing down at the floor, she whispered, "Eric. His BMW is gone! I think it was stolen."

JD took Kalldah's hand and pulled her out the door. JD whipped out his cell phone as they raced down the hallway, down the stairs, and through the lobby. The cement stung Kalldah's bare feet as she hopped down the streets of Tavern. Kalldah bit down on her bottom lip to stop from screaming. But it wasn't enough. JD stopped dead in his tracks, and gave Kalldah a piggyback ride.

JD called the police, ordering them to meet him at Interstate 64. "Heading east or west?" The operator asked him. "I don't know," he replied.

Once JD, Kalldah, and the police had arrived at the Interstate, they began to search up and down the freeway, and back again. They spotted no sign of a crash anywhere.

The officers questioned JD and Kalldah.

JD's Interview:

"Who is the victim?"

"Kalldah Farland."

"What did she tell you happened?"

"She told me that she crashed Eric Bulvernans BMW on Interstate 64."

"Are you a witness of this?"

"No sir. I was not at the scene of the accident. I found Kalldah locked in a room at Days Inn on 55th and Tavern."

"How long ago was this?"

"Only an hour ago sir. I dialed for the police on my way up here."

"Okay. Anything else to assist us with the investigation?"

"Yes. I believe there is. Ummm... Kalldah kept mentioning that something went missing?"

"Did she happen to say who or what? And when it went missing?"

"No. I suppose it happened at the time the crash occured. But she left me with no hint as to who or what went missing."

"Okay sir that will be all."

"Wait!" The officer turned.

"Yes, Mr. Branson?"

"There is one thing, I almost forgot! The BMW! She told me the BMW was gone."

Interview with Kalldah:

"Full name miss?"

"Kalldah Sharee Farland."

"Tell me everything you know, so we can help you."

"I crashed Eric's car. I ran and I ran... I had to go. I don't know what happened. Out of nowhere, it came. Everything went black."

"Do you remember anything else?"

Kalldah shook her head no.

"Can you tell me how you got to the hotel?"

"Yes, I remember! I remember Eric dragging me away from the car to the hotel. I don't know... But I remember waking up in a dark hotel room with no key. I was alone!" Kalldah shuttered.

The officer's eyes widened, and he asked Kalldah, "So it was Eric who dragged you to the hotel?"

"Yes. It was."

"Okay, so how did you crash Eric's car? Who's car was he driving when the accident happened?"

"Sir, Eric called me this morning. He told me that JD planned to take me on a special date today. He said JD requested that he be my chauffer. So I agreed. I drove my car to Eric's house. I didn't want my mother to question me about why Eric was picking me up and not JD himself."

"Wait!" The officer held up a finger. "What is Eric's relationship with JD?"

"They're close friends."

"What is JD to you?"

"He's my boyfriend of course."

"Okay, so what happened next? And don't leave out any details."

"Eric was waiting outside as I drove up his driveway. When I got out of the car, he came over to me, and grabbed me. He forced me into his BMW. Somehow I managed to get out of his grip. I climbed from the back seat to the front seat and drove off before Eric could stop me. Eric took my car, and came after me. He called me on his cell, from my car, and told me to go to Days Inn. I didn't have anywhere else to go, so I did what he said. So once we got to Days Inn... Look, I told you what I remember. I woke up alone, in a dark hotel room."

"Where is your car now?"

"I don't know. It should be still parked in the hotel's parking lot where I left it."

"Were you with or without a driver's license at the time of your getaway?"

"Uhh..." Kalldah stammered. "I think I left my purse in my car. Or it may be in the BMW."

"Okay miss, I'm going to have an officer take you back to the hotel. I want you to check your car, and grab your purse if it's there. Then you will be brought down to the station. We'll need your full statement. There's a chance that Eric and JD will be on trial, but we will need you there as a witness."

"Okay. Okay, sir."

"And! If your purse is not there, then you may be fined for driving without a license."

Officer Landry drove Kalldah back to the hotel, and escorted her to her car. Luckily Kalldah found her purse lying in the passenger's seat of her car, untouched as she'd left it.

At the police station, she had to make a phone call to her parents, in the presence of an officer. It was agonizing for her to explain to them why she was at a police station. After all that Kalldah had through in the past, their patience had been worn out. They no longer were capable of being understanding. At least not in a troubling circumstance, such as this.

Kalldah's parents came down to the station immediately. Before they could take Kalldah home, they too were questioned on events that had taken place before the accident. Mr. and Mrs. Farland just sat in their seats, looking dumbfounded. Officer Landry looked discouraged, and finally released them. She re-assured both parents that Kalldah was simply a witness. She was not going to be held in police custody any longer. Each of Kalldah's parents let out a sigh of relief as they left the premises.

Hate has a strange way of corrupting love. It's clear to see who the mastermind of all this is. Surely there has to be a reasonable explanation for this. It's by the grace of God that... didn't follow through. No man can justify the means of another. Every man, full of lies and deceit has a mind of his own. Only he truly knows the remedies of his heart.

One man's loss, leaves another man stricken. In this case it happens to be a woman. Kalldah remains blind to the facts, and fails to realize the afflictions she may bare. Because she does not know, she is unable to abort. It'd be wise of her to quickly remove herself from this. Abandoning all JD has to offer.

The devilish creature clings to Kalldah with its claws of hate. It whisks her away on the wings of love. A premature love. A meaningless love. A pointless, useless love, and a doubtful love. Leaving one with many questions unanswered.

For Kalldah it's too late. The past we cannot undo. If I could've warned her, then I would have said, "Kalldah, love is not sex, and sex is not love." Cause once you give of yourself, there is no getting it back. Forever you'll regret, and there is nothing to fill that void. Maybe she'll find true love. Maybe. But "maybe" is not for certain. In the end, who walks away with what they wanted from the very beginning? JD. Who leaves in sorrow? Kalldah.

What does hate have to do with this? Hate is the master of this all. For hate is the opposite of love. If it was real love from the genesis, then Kalldah never would have been abused. She wouldn't have given, only to lose. For every cause there is an effect. This cause is hate (fake love, lust, deceit), the effect is denial and...

Mr. Farland grumbled and complained all the way home. Kalldah sat in the backseat of her father's car, with her arms folded against her chest.

"How could you allow this to happen Kalldah?" Mrs. Farland questioned.

"It was an accident!" replied Kalldah.

"Why can't you take your car? What's wrong with it?" asked Mr. Farland.

"They want to search it. To see if they can get any more information, or evidence to back up my statement," Kalldah answered.

"How did JD know where to find you?" Mrs. Farland asked curiously.

"Yes, how did he?" Mr. Farland pressed.

"I don't know!" Kalldah quickly replied. "We were suppose to meet at the hotel. He was going to take me out on a date."

"Why couldn't he have picked you up from the house himself?" Mr. Farland asked.

Mrs. Farland said, "I never trusted that boy! After what he did to you? I don't know why you got back with him!"

Mr. Farland had his say on the issue as well. He said, "Kalldah, I want you to stay away from him, you hear me? Stay away! And you let him know."

Later that day Kalldah's parents received a phone call from the police station. Officer Landry said that they had a detective awaiting more information.

Mrs. Farland knocked on Kalldah's bedroom door. Kalldah opened up, and asked "What now?" "Sorry to interrupt your little nap, but you have to go back to the station. They want to test you for drugs."

Down at the police station Kalldah was tested to see if any drugs remained in her system. They discovered that she'd been drugged indeed. The detective, Danny Orega, pulled out his note pad and began questioning Kalldah.

"Full name please, with middle initial."

"Kalldah S. Farland."

"What happened at the hotel?"

"Eric dragged me up the stairs and into a room. I remember it was very dark. The next thing I know, I was waking up, lying on the floor, alone."

"So you say that you woke up correct?"

"Yes. I was alone too," Kalldah confirmed.

"You've been tested for drugs. Did you take anything intentionally, before you left for the hotel? Any Tylenol? Or anything that is capable of making you drowsy?" Detective Orega asked.

"No, I'm sure I didn't."

"Do you have any idea why this Eric took you to that hotel room, and left you alone in the dark?"

"Not really! No, I mean, I was supposed to be meeting JD outside in the hotel parking lot."

The detective hesitated. He scribbled down a few more notes. Then he looked up at Kalldah sternly and said, "I'm going to go take another look at those test results. But I think what we have here is a case of date rape."

"Date rape?" Kalldah asked out of confusion.

"Yes, are you familiar with the drug at all? Do you know what it's used for?"

"Yea... I think I understand now. He was trying to get me into bed! He was trying to get me to sleep with him! I can't believe him!"

Kalldah had been given the opportunity to believe. The one thing that seems to be farthest from the truth may be the one thing that could save a life.

"Who? Kalldah who?"

"JD. JD Branson. He's my boyfriend."

"I take it you had no idea he was behind all this?"

"Of course not!" Kalldah exclaimed.

Kalldah believed what she wanted to believe. She continuously listened to the lies JD told her. Fact is, she was well aware of what JD was capable of doing. If a man is willing to lie once, he's willing to do it again and again. That's what hate does. Hate is not capable of loving. JD had hurt Kalldah once, it's no surprise that he'd done it again. At least it shouldn't be a surprise.

Only the wise shall survive. There will be the five wise and the five foolish. She was tempted and tried, and she failed to survive. You would think that one would be cautious. At least a little observant. But no! Not Kalldah. She had to block out her past, and move forward, because she was taught that, that was the right thing to do. And it is. So long as you are not carrying along excess baggage.

Leaving the past behind you is a positive thing. The mistake Kalldah made, was going back to her past. Once you go back, you have a less chance of making it out alive.

Like those who are unready for death, they are often snatched from the land of the living unwillingly. Kalldah was snatched up by hate. She willfully rejected salvation, by refusing to believe. Refusing to believe the facts of this reality. This reality being that JD does not truly love her.

I Was Wrong

Roses are black
Violets are red
Sexy and fine is what came to my mind
But I have found out
That you are malicious
My view has changed
Every time I saw you
I use to be dazed
But now I'm alert
I'm no longer amazed
You captivated my mind
It was almost fate
Karma is what I believe
But this I don't
You did this to me
By breaking my heart
If I was a queen
Then you'd be gone
I am only a young girl
So I'll just be mature
I am not delirious, nor am I confused
I remember what happened
Every order, every step
I must have been psycho
To desire your flame
You did not deserve
My spice and rare savory
Cause when I first saw you

I not only saw charm, but affection
I gave you my devotion
I know you are sitting back, laughing
But you was drop dead gorgeous
Now you're just scum
Un-tamed and unbalanced
That is what you are
And if you don't think I will forget
Then you should know now, that I won't
I will now and forever remain
Cherishing admiration
Of what use to be
You.

You Are My Nightmare

You're my nightmare, want to know why?
Maybe it's cause your hidden beneath a disguise
And every word you utter tends to be a lie
Every time I try to talk about us
All your concerned about is lust
Love is just a game to you
You'll do anything, so you don't lose
Forever and always you abuse, my friendship
Every word you said, was a part of your little trick

Pain and sorrow should bring tears to your eyes
But it doesn't
That's why you're the one I despise
After all that I've given up
Finally I realize your only bad luck
Because my life has gone to waste
Now my heart is filled with hate
Some say it's only fate
And to reverse it, it's too late
I can never forget
So today and tomorrow
And for the rest of my life
You are my nightmare.

Chapter Five

About a good month later, after a trial date had been set, Kalldah began to go into a deep depression. She began to fade in to the pale walls of her bedroom. Rarely did she eat, or go outside.

Once again her heart was broken. She was fooled by hate... Maybe she did love him, maybe she didn't. Love blinds. So no-one truly knows. But when two truly love each other, then they'll know for certain. And those who are on the outside looking in will clearly see... They say you don't truly know, until you've experienced it for yourself. That's just the way love is. When love is given, it's up to one to except it. Or you can make a mistake, like Kalldah did. She excepted a love that was not real. A love in disguise is hate.

Someone can buy on original Gucci bag from the department store. Another person can purchase a remake of the original thing. That's how love is in this story. Kalldah's story is a representation of this. The wheels turn in the same way. Yet it all runs backwards.

Soon the day of the trial arrived. Kalldah, her parents, the lawyer, and officer Landry were present. Kalldah sat quietly in the witness booth, as officer Landry stood beside her. Kalldah's parents had an awkward expression on their faces. Almost as if they'd murder a man if the trial didn't go their way. Judge Mandino waited patiently, his eyes glued to JD and Eric, as they walked into the room. Both JD and Eric seemed uncomfortable, because their hands were handcuffed behind their backs.

Finally court began...

All evidence pointed at JD and Eric, proving that they were guilty. JD's lawyer had a tough time defending JD. That became very obvious. Judge Mandino requested to view Kalldah's test results.

"Here at the bottom, a doctor has signed these results as confirmation. So far I have little reason to believe that this is not a case of date rape."

Kalldah's lawyer called her to the witness stand.

"Miss Farland why were you at the hotel that morning?"

"Eric told me that JD wanted to take me somewhere special on our date. Later I was trying to escape from Eric, but I ended up driving his car. He called me on my cell and told me to meet him at Day's Inn. I had nowhere else to go, so I did," Kalldah declared.

"Mr. Branson, was the accident a set up?"

"No," JD replied carelessly.

"Your honor, JD contacted the police himself, informing them of the accident. Officer Landry here, was there as well. No evidence could be found, that there'd been a crash of any kind."

"Who's car was involved in the accident Mr. Branson?" Judge Mandino asked.

"Eric's and Kalldah's."

"Sir, we kept Kalldah's car for further inspection. There were no scratches, or dents found on the vehicle."

"So there was no accident?" Judge Mandino asked.

"That is the very point we are trying to prove," Kalldah's lawyer said.

"Therefore Mr. Branson here is guilty. His lying and scheming also involves Eric. So they are both sentenced to six months in the county jail."

And with that, Judge Mandino confirmed his decision, and court was over.

The last time Kalldah was hurt by JD, it was from physical abuse. Of course she didn't only suffer physically, but emotionally as well. When Kalldah and JD first met, they were in high school. They both attended Southern Atlantic High School, and sat in the back of Mrs. Johnsons Economy class during fifth period. JD was automatically attracted to Kalldah's physical appearance. He didn't know the first thing about Kalldah. He did at least know her first name. That was all he needed to know, to make his first move. In fact, knowing her name wasn't even all that necessary. So JD quickly asked Kalldah out. Kalldah was instantly in awe of JD's good looks. She was mesmerized by his sparkling blue eyes, lightly-tanned skin, thick strands of blonde hair draping over his left eye, his charming smile, and his handsomeness.

His tone was deep, smooth, and cunning. He captured Kalldah from the very beginning. JD Branson held Kalldah Sharee Farland in the palm of his sweaty, blistery hand.

It causes her great shame, that she was fooled by this man. She tripped and fell in what she thought was love. From their very first date, the couple bonded. Kalldah was happier than ever. The love she thought she had for him was only lust.

JD only wanted one thing from Kalldah. He was willing to steal away the precious gift given to women at birth. The one gift that one cannot get back, ever. Hate, selfishness, and greed... I dislike having to tell this part of the story. I will make this as short and simple as possible. JD tried to rape Kalldah, when they'd first started dating. Kalldah was foolish enough to listen to his lies. I must say that she's had good luck in being able to escape. Though she was strong enough to endure and escape, she is too weak to live and let live. Now she can't find her passion, and live her dream. She confided in me multiple times. I listened to her. But the one thing she would not do is hear me out.

This is nothing but a tragedy. A love story without a happy ending. You would have thought that JD and Eric being sent to jail would be closure. Maybe now she'd walk away for good. But as I have stated many times before, it is too late.

Kalldah did not listen to her parents, Dr. McKay, or me. The date rape case sent Kalldah spiraling into a deep, deep, deep depression. Hate haunts her in the night. She cannot block the memories of her past that haunts her too. The word that JD whispered in her ears rehearses itself in her memory. I say all this to say... Kalldah has forever dreamt of having a fairytale love life. But when reality strikes, she realizes the truth. Though love is a beautiful thing, sometimes hate comes and destroys it all.

She is broken
She is needy
She is blind
Love is beautiful
It is hate that ruined her life.

Love and hate cannot be combined. Hate is love's enemy, and it's victim will suffer the consequences. Kalldah suffered emotionally, because she failed to understand what love truly is. Kalldah's testimony is simply a tragic love story. A fairytale without a happy ending. Love blinds. But it is the blind that has opened mine eyes that I may see.

This is not just the ending of Kalldah's tragic love story. But this is also the beginning of a greater love...

Love Is a Beautiful Thing

Sometimes love hurts
But that will never change
How beautiful love can be
Never confuse love with lust…
Be sure that your love is true love.

Afterword

Kalldah's parents finally decide that it may be best that Kalldah goes back to the rehabilitation center. There she rooms with Trinity, and they become close friends. Kalldah works with Dr. McKay, and soon she learns to forgive JD. A few months later, Dr. McKay feels that Kalldah is not only ready to leave rehab, but she is also ready for the next big step. Dr. McKay allows Kalldah to go and visit JD in jail as much as she'd like. Kalldah and JD do not get back together, but it seems that JD has changed as a person. He admits to the mistakes he has made and is willing to just be friends.

Sereyva still keeps in contact with Kalldah. They aren't as close as they were before Kalldah was sent to rehab, but they still communicate. Things really seem to be looking up for these young girls. They have learned the difference between a fairytale love, and true love. Romance is one of the most beautiful things any of them could ever wish to experience. They have also found a greater love…

They searched for love in all the wrong places
Every crack and every corner
None of them having what they were in need of

They thought they needed a warm body beside them
And an arm to be wrapped around them

But...

1 John 4: 7-8 and 11-12 says,

Beloved, let us love one another, for love is of God; and every one that loveth is born of God, and knoweth God.

He that loveth not, knoweth not God; for God is love.

Beloved, if God so loved us, we ought to love one another.

... If we love one another, God dwelleth in us, and his love is perfected in us.

So love is beautiful. Hate is ugly. It's as simple as that.

Find that one special person, and fall in TRUE love. Surely you won't regret it. Ever.

About the Author

Kezia Arterberry was born in the hot, Arizona summer of 1993. She has been writing, poetry, and songs since she was a little girl. And she has also received various awards and certificates for her short stories and poetry. Kezia has developed a passion and joy for not only writing, but music as well. Singing and writing inspirational lyrics has always been her leisure pursuit. There are many people who have inspired her to strive for perfection, by reaching and achieving her dreams in life. Including: Rutha & Marcus Arterberry, Dorcus C. Chandler, Jasmine Richerdson, Tori A. Sims, Mary J. Blige, Raven Symone, Tyra Banks, Michael Jackson, Kurt Warner, and many others. After graduating she hopes to continue striving for perfection. She plans to attend a four year university majoring in music therapy, and minor in creative writing. Then she hopes to transfer to an all music school, pursuing a degree in Voice.

- Nobody knows what the future holds. We can only hope, pray, and dream that great things are to come. (Kezia)